This book belongs to

....

MURILLA GORILLA
AND THE LOST PARASOL
JENNIFER LLOYD
ILLUSTRATED BY JACQUI LEE
SIMPLY READ BOOKS
WITHDRAWN

To my dear friend, Claudine. —J. Lloyd

Published in 2013 by Simply Read Books
www.simplyreadbooks.com

Library and Archives Canada Cataloguing in Publication
Lloyd, Jennifer
Murilla gorilla and the lost parasol / written by Jennifer Lloyd; with illustrations by Jacqui Lee.

ISBN 978-1-927018-23-1

I. Lee, Jacqui II. Title.

PS8623.L69M875 2013 jC813´.6 C2013-900911-6

We gratefully acknowledge for their financial support of our publishing program the Canada Council for the Arts, the BC Arts Council, and the Government of Canada through the Canada Book Fund (CBF).

Manufactured in Malaysia

Book design by Naomi MacDougall

10 9 8 7 6 5 4 3 2 1

Contents

ZZZZ

Chapter 1
Puddles

PITTER! PATTER! PITTER! PATTER!

It rained all night in the African Rainforest. At last, the rain stopped.

Murilla Gorilla woke up.
She got out of bed.

SPLASH! She stepped into a puddle.

"Uh-oh! The rain leaked through my roof."

Murilla looked for her mop
in her messy hut.

She checked under her table.

Not there.

She checked in her oven.

Not there.

Murilla found her mop.
It was in her bathtub!

Oops! The handle fell off.

The mop was old. Murilla needed to buy a new one.

She got ready to go to Mango Market.

Murilla is a detective. She never knows when she will have to solve a mystery.

Just in case, she brought her detective backpack.

Murilla stepped outside.

Puddles were everywhere.

Murilla drove down the mountain.
Lizard was on the side of the road.
SPLASH!

"Watch out!" cried Murilla. Too late!

Lizard got soaked.

At last, she pulled into Mango Market.

SH FRUIT
SALE!

Chapter 2
A New Case

Murilla headed straight to Mandrill's Mops.

"Mops are on special today," Mandrill said.

Murilla looked at the mops.

Murilla picked up a mop with a long handle.

Something tickled her shoulder.

She picked up a mop with a short handle.

Something tickled her shoulder again.

"Sorry, Parrot. I did not see you there."

"Murilla, I have a case for you. Something is missing from my parasol stand. Will you help me find it?" asked Parrot.

"I'll be right there," said Murilla.

But Murilla never liked to rush.

Murilla picked up the mop with the long handle again.

"Should I buy this one?" she asked Parrot.

"Murilla! I need you!"

"Right," said Murilla.

PARROT'S
PARASOLS

Chapter Three
Backpack Surprise

Murilla followed Parrot to his stand.

Parrot's parasols were a mess.

"How can I help?" Murilla asked.

"My yellow parasol is missing," explained Parrot.

"Where did it go?"

"Murilla! That's what I want you to find out!"

"Right! I'll check for footprints."

Murilla opened her backpack. She hunted for her magnifying glass.

She pulled out something round with a handle.

"Murilla, that's a frying pan!"

When Murilla reached in again, something jumped out.

"Tree Frog! What are you doing in my backpack?"

"The trees are too wet. I needed a dry place to sleep."

"Out you go, Tree Frog. Murilla has work to do," Parrot said.

At last, Murilla found her magnifying glass.

Chapter 4
Mysterious Tracks

Murilla walked to the left of Parrot's Parasols. She looked through her magnifying glass.

She did not see any footprints.

Murilla turned around. She walked to the right. This time she saw tracks.

"Aha! These must belong to the parasol thief!"

"Murilla, those are your footprints," said Parrot.

Murilla was embarrassed.

GRRR! Her tummy rumbled. She had forgotten to eat breakfast!

"Maybe a snack will help me solve this case."

Magnificent
SALE!

Chapter 5
Yellow Things

"Banana muffin?" asked Ms. Chimpanzee.

"Sure." Murilla took a muffin.

"This muffin tastes different," said Murilla.

"The muffins got wet in the storm," said Ms. Chimpanzee.

Murilla was hungry. She ate it anyway.

She felt a tickle on her shoulder again.

"Murilla, why aren't you looking for my yellow parasol?" asked Parrot.

"Oops!"

Murilla took out her notebook.
She drew a picture of the parasol.

But Murilla did not know what to do next.

“Can I have another muffin?” she asked Ms. Chimpanzee.

“Murilla, why don’t you go look for yellow things?” said Ms. Chimpanzee.

“Good idea.”

Murilla saw something yellow at Okapi's Hammocks.

It was a beach towel. Okapi was using it to dry off his wet hammocks.

"Wet hammocks are on sale today," said Okapi.

"No thanks," said Murilla.

Murilla walked to Hippo's Hot Tubs.

Hippo was busy. She was emptying water from a hot tub. The storm had made it too full.

Murilla looked in the tub. She did not see anything yellow.

Chapter 6
SWISH! SWISH!

Murilla walked back to
Parrot's Parasols.

She opened her backpack.
She took out a giant fan.

SWISH! SWISH! Murilla waved
the fan around Parrot's Parasols.

"What are you doing?"
asked Parrot.

SWISH! SWISH!
Murilla waved the fan again.

"Murilla!"

"Shh! I am pretending to be the wind."

"How will that help you catch the parasol thief?"

"I don't think that there is a parasol thief! I think that the wind blew your parasol away."

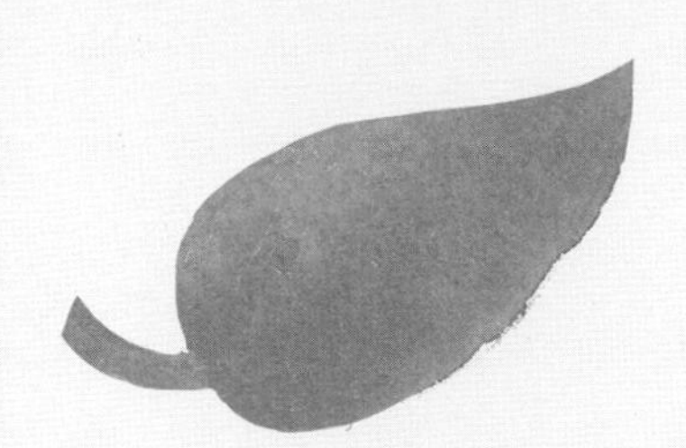

SWISH! SWISH!
Murilla waved faster.

This time a leaf on
the ground blew up
in the air!

Murilla looked up.

Something was stuck
in the tree branches.

Murilla climbed up.

Soon she could see what was stuck in the tree.

It was big. It was yellow.

"Parrot's parasol!"

"Zzzz."

Murilla heard a sound.
She peeked in.

Inside was Tree Frog, fast asleep.

Chapter 7
Back Home

Murilla climbed down.
She was tired.

She drove back to her
hut to take a nap.

SPLASH! Murilla stepped in the
puddle beside her bed.

Oops! Murilla had forgotten
to bring home a mop.

Murilla did not care.
She climbed under the covers.

"Zzzz!"

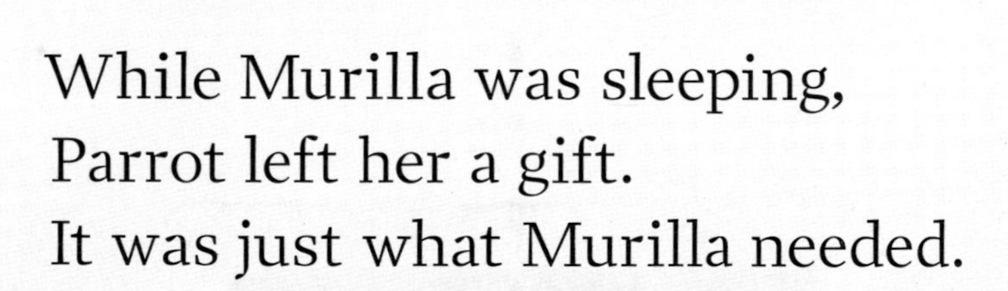

While Murilla was sleeping,
Parrot left her a gift.
It was just what Murilla needed.